If I Ran the Circus was originally cataloged by the Library of Congress as follows:
Geisel, Theodor Seuss. If I ran the circus, by Dr. Seuss [pseud.]
New York, Random House [1956] I. Title. PZ8.G276ld 56-9469
ISBN: 0-394-80080-X (trade) ; 0-394-90080-4 (lib. bdg.) ; 0-394-84546-3 (pbk.)

If I Ran the Zoo was originally cataloged by the Library of Congress as follows:
Geisel, Theodor Seuss. If I ran the zoo, by Dr. Seuss {pseud.}
New York, Random House {1950} I. Title. PZ8.3G276If 50-10185
ISBN: 0-394-80081-8 (trade hardcover) ; 0-394-90081-2 (library binding)

Printed in the United States of America   10 9 8 7 6 5 4 3 2 1

www.randomhouse.com/kids/
www.randomhouse.com/seussville/

"**In all** the whole town, the most wonderful spot
Is behind Sneelock's Store in the big vacant lot.
It's *just* the right spot for my wonderful plans,"
Said young Morris McGurk, "...if I clean up the cans."

"Now a fellow like me," said young Morris McGurk,
"Could get rid of this junk with a half hour's work.
I could yank up those weeds. And chop down the dead tree.
And haul off those old cars. There are just two or three.
And *then* the whole place would be ready, you see . . ."

All ready to put up the tents for my circus.
I think I will call it the Circus McGurkus.

The Circus McGurkus! The World's Greatest Show
On the face of the earth, or wherever you go!

The Circus McGurkus! The cream of the cream!
The Circus McGurkus! The Circus Supreme!
The Circus McGurkus! Colossal! Stupendous!
Astounding! Fantastic! Terrific! Tremendous!
I'll bring in my acrobats, jugglers and clowns
From a thousand and thirty-three faraway towns
To the place that you'll see 'em in, ladies and gents,
Right behind Sneelock's Store, in the Great McGurk tents!

And I don't suppose old Mr. Sneelock will mind
When he suddenly has a big circus behind...

After all, Mr. Sneelock is one of my friends.
He might even help out doing small odds and ends.
Doing little odd jobs, he could be of some aid...
Such as selling balloons and the pink lemonade.
I think five hundred gallons will be about right.
And THEN, I'll be ready for Opening Night!

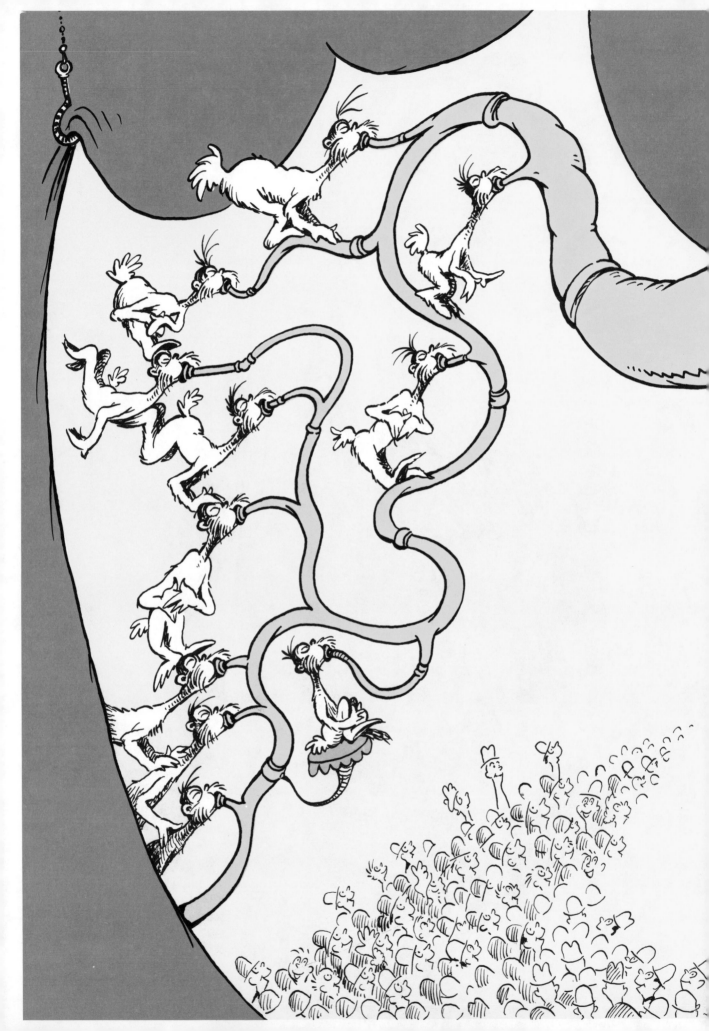

What an Opening Night!
What a night!
What a sight!

I'll hoist up the curtains! The crowds will crowd in!
And my Circus McGurkus will promptly begin
With a welcoming toot on my Welcoming Horn
By my horn-tooting apes from the Jungles of Jorn
Where the very best horn-tooting apes are all born
'Cause the very fresh air there is fine for their lungs.
And some of those fellows have two or three tongues!

This way! Step right in! This way, ladies and gents!
My Side Show starts here in the first of my tents.
When you see what goes on, you'll say no other circus is
Half the great circus the Circus McGurkus is.
Here on Stage One, from the Ocean of Olf
Is a sight most amazing—a walrus named Rolf
Who can stand on *one whisker,* this wonderful Rolf,
On the top of five balls! Two for tennis, three golf.
It's a marvelous trick, if I say so mysolf.

And on Stage Number Two
Here is something quite new!

From a country called Frumm
Comes this Drum-Tummied Snumm
Who can drum any tune
That you might care to hum.
(Doesn't hurt him a bit
Cause his Drum-Tummy's numb.)

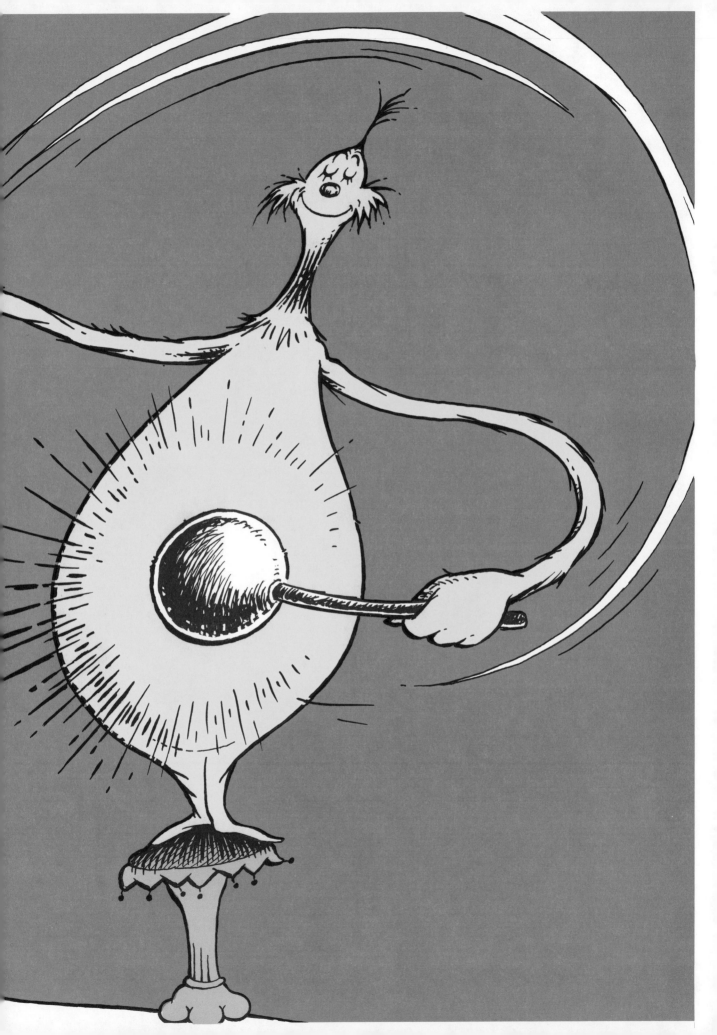

And you'll now meet the Foon! The Remarkable Foon
Who eats sizzling hot pebbles that fall off the moon!
And the reason he likes them red hot, it appears,
Is he greatly enjoys blowing smoke from his ears.

Of course pebbles like this are quite hard to collect
But Sneelock will manage, somehow, I expect.
After all, Mr. Sneelock is one of my friends
And I'm sure he'll help out doing small odds and ends.

And on Stage Number Four, see the Wily Walloo
Who can throw his long tail as a sort of lassoo!
With a flip of the hip, with a tail of this kind
He can capture whoever is standing behind!
He can capture old Sneelock. I'm sure he won't mind.

And now here is a Hoodwink
Who winks in his wink-hood.
Without a good wink-hood
A Hoodwink can't wink good.
And, folks, let me tell you
There's only *one* circus
With wink-hooded Hoodwinks!
The Circus McGurkus!

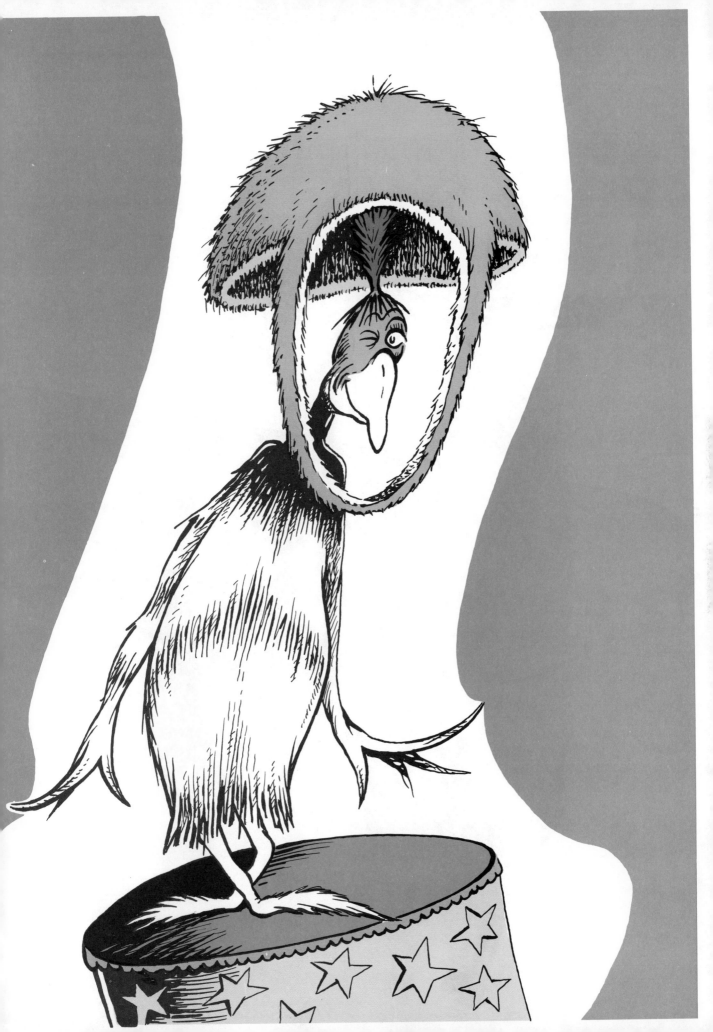

The Show of All Shows!

There's no other Showman

Who shows you a show with a Blindfolded Bowman!

The Blindfolded Bowman from Brigger-ba-Root,

The world's sharpest sharpshooter. *Look* at him shoot!

Through the holes in four doughnuts!

Two hairs on a worm!

And the knees of three birds

Without making them squirm!

And, then, on through a crab apple up on the head

Of Sneelock, who likes to help out, as I've said.

And, now, come to this spot
Where the spotlight is hot
And you'll see in the spotlight
A Juggling Jott
Who can juggle some stuff
You might think he could not . . .
Such as twenty-two question marks,
Which is a lot.
Also forty-four commas
And, *also,* one dot!
That's the kind of a Circus McGurkus I've got!

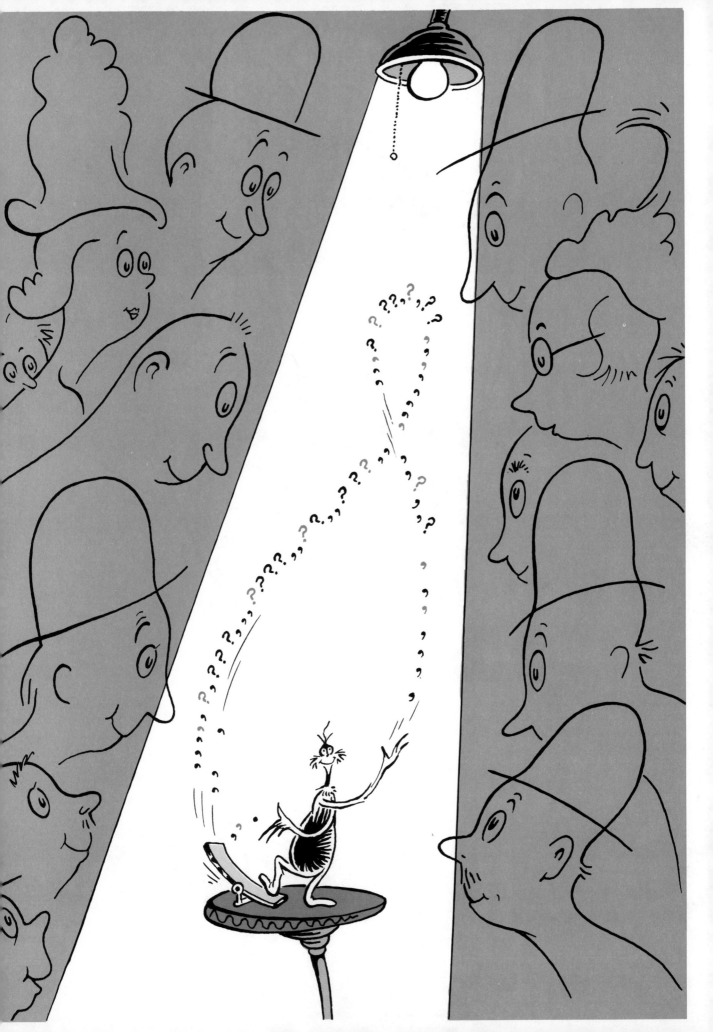

But that's just my Side Show. A start. A beginning.
This way to the Big Tent! You'll find your head spinning.
Why, ladies and gentlemen, youngsters and oldsters,
Your heads will quite likely spin right off your shouldsters!
So hurry! Step lively! Quick, ladies and gents!
And get in to your seats in my Tent-of-all-Tents!
My Parade-of-Parades is about to commence!

You'll see Drum Major Sneelock fling-flang his baton
And my Organ-McOrgan-McGurkus come on
With its hot steaming pipes of gold brass-plated tin
Snorting all sorts of snorts in a bummbeling din
That is super-Stoo-Pendus! Stoo-Mendus! Stoo-Roarus!
And, when I play *Dixie,* please join in the chorus.

Then a fluff-muffled Truffle will ride on a Huffle
And, next in the line, a fine Flummox will shuffle.
The Flummox will carry a Lurch in a pail
And a Fibbel will carry the Flummox's tail
While, on top of the Flummox, three Harp-Twanging Snarp
Will twang mighty twangs on their Three-Snarper-Harp
While a Bolster blows bloops on a three-nozzled bloozer!
A Nolster blows floops on a one-nozzled noozer!
And *then* comes a lion who's partly a trout!
Then *more* stuff! For forty-five minutes, about!

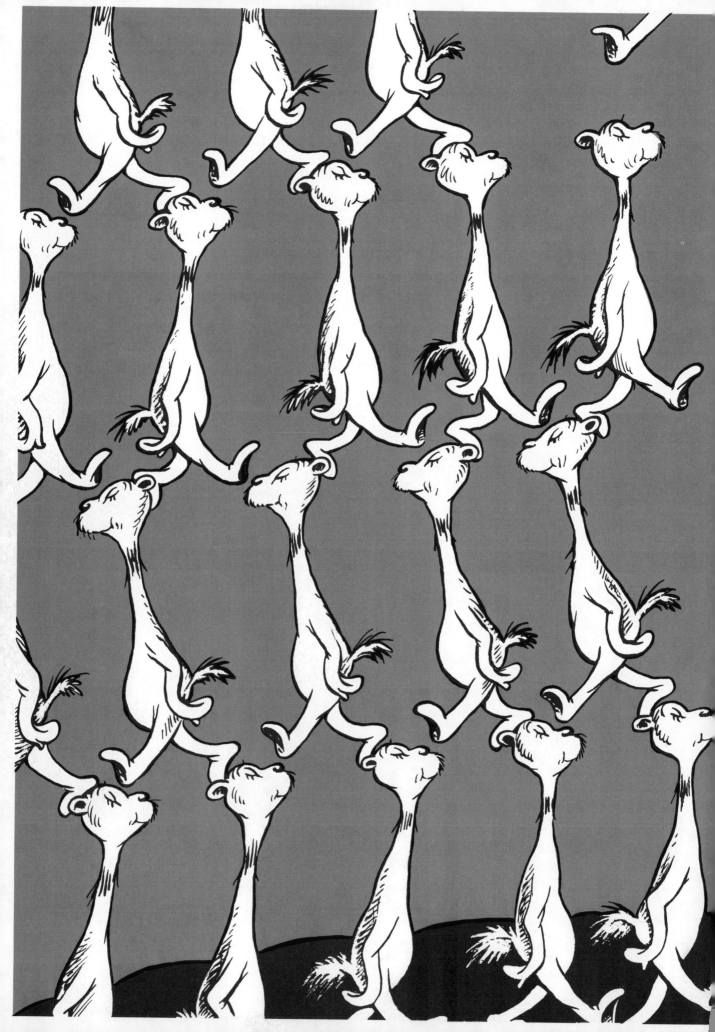

And THEN, behind *them*, then,
While everyone stares
Come my To-an-Fro Marchers
Who march in five layers!
The Fros march on Tos
And the Tos march on Fros.
Don't know how they do it,
But that's how it goes.

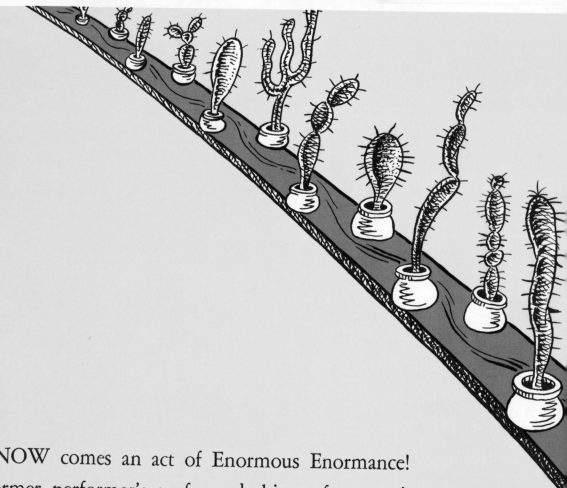

And NOW comes an act of Enormous Enormance!
No former performer's performed this performance!
This stunt is too grippingly, slippingly fright'ning!
DOWN from the top of my tent like greased lightning
Through pots full of lots of big Stickle-Bush Trees
Slides a man! What a man! On his Roller-Skate-Skis!
And he'll steer without fear and you'll know at a glance
That it's Sneelock! The Man who takes chance after chance!
And he won't even rip a small hole in his pants.

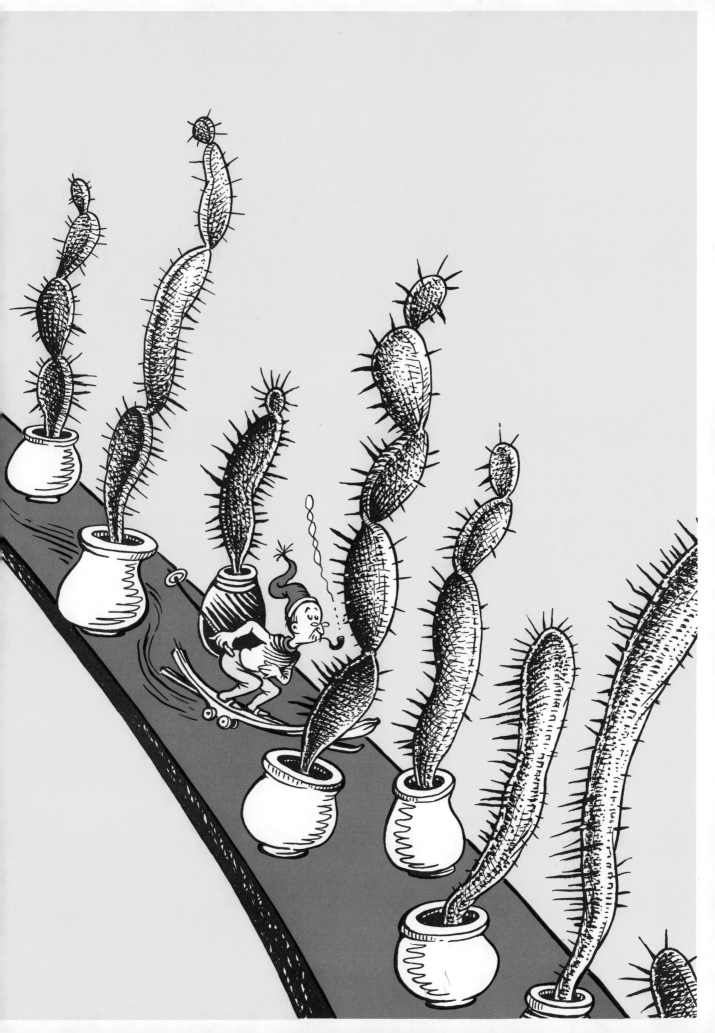

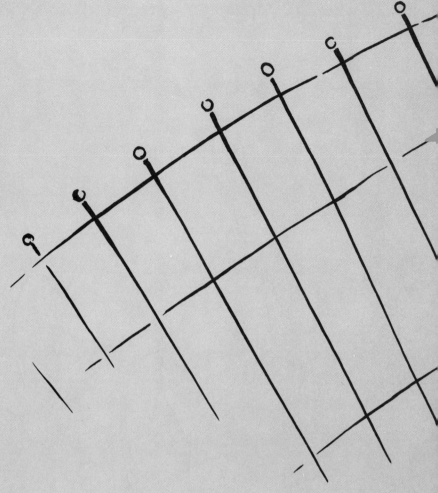

And now *Here!*
In this cage
Is a beast most ferocious
Who's known far and wide
As the Spotted Atrocious
Who growls, howls and yowls
The most bloodcurdling sounds
And each tooth in his mouth
Weighs at least sixty pounds
And he chews up and eats with the greatest of ease
Things like carpets and sidewalks and people and trees!
But the great Colonel Sneelock is just the right kind
Of a man who can tame him. I'm sure he won't mind.

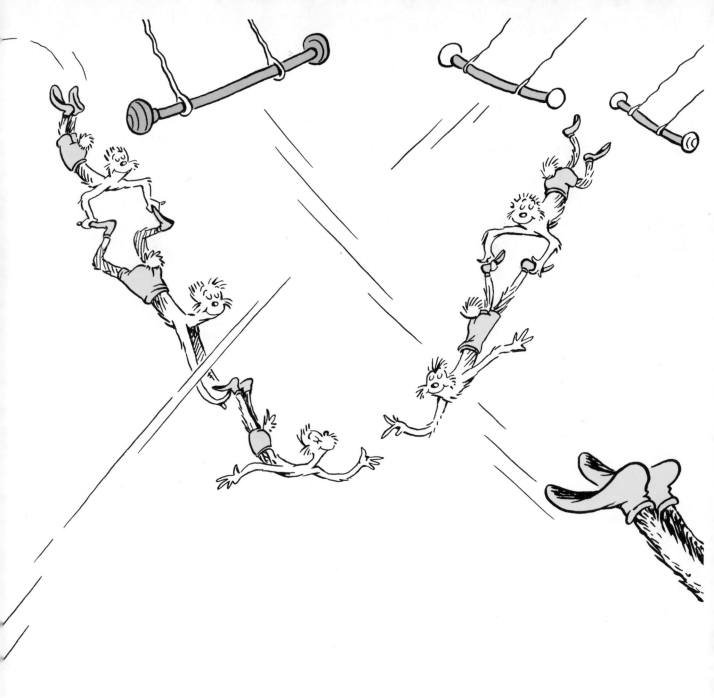

Then I'll let Sneelock off for a few minutes' rest
While high over your heads you will see the best best
Of the world's finest, fanciest Breezy Trapeezing!
My Zoom-a-Zoop Troupe from West Upper Ben-Deezing
Who never quite know, while they zoop and they zoom,
Whether which will catch what one, or who will catch whom
Or if who will catch which by the what and just where,
Or just when and just how in which part of the air!

Ei! Ei! What a circus! My Circus McGurkus!
My workers *love* work. They say, "Work us! Please work us!
We'll work and we'll work up so many surprises
You'd never see half if you had forty eyses!"

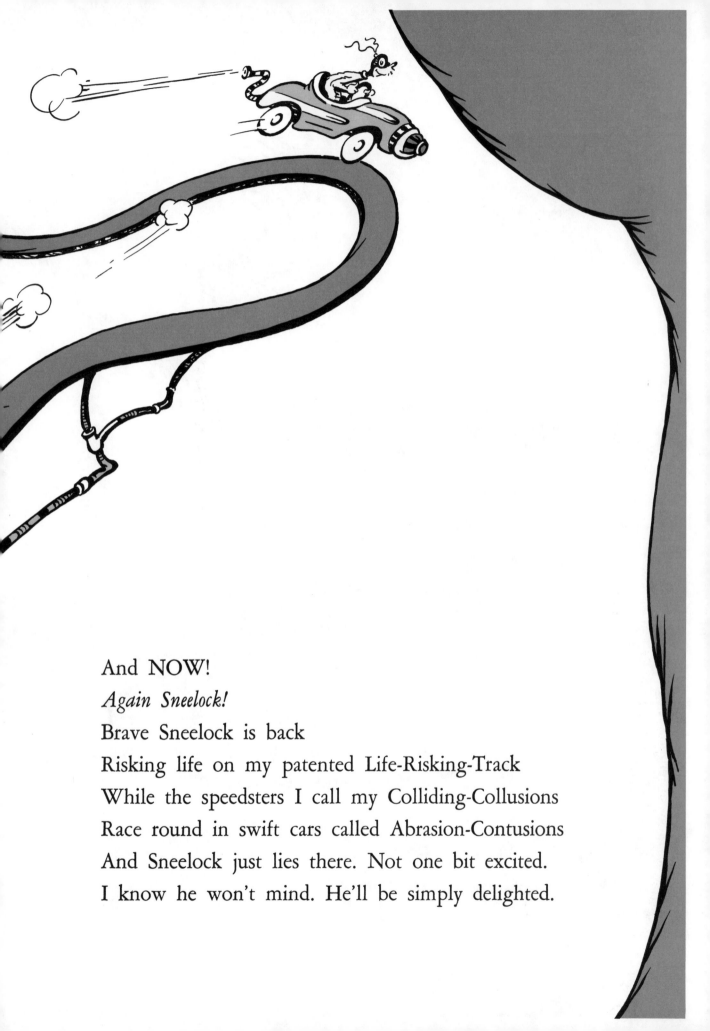

And NOW!
Again Sneelock!
Brave Sneelock is back
Risking life on my patented Life-Risking-Track
While the speedsters I call my Colliding-Collusions
Race round in swift cars called Abrasion-Contusions
And Sneelock just lies there. Not one bit excited.
I know he won't mind. He'll be simply delighted.

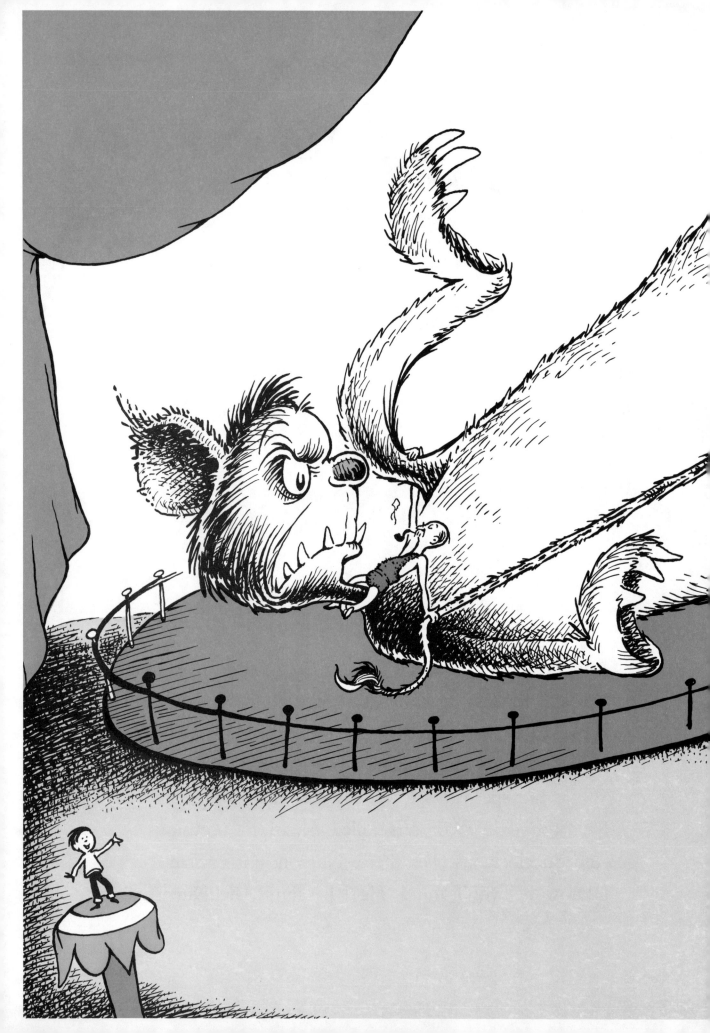

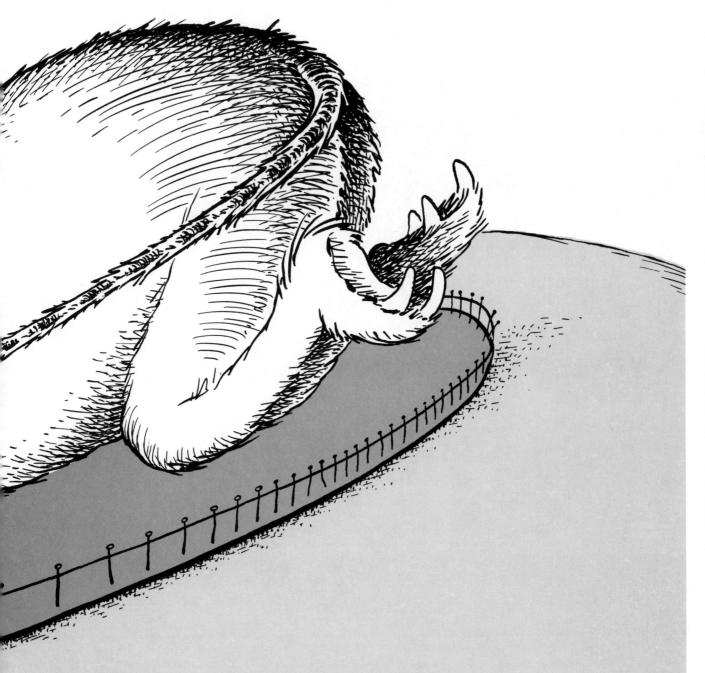

And *here,* in a contest of brute-strength and muscle,
Kid Sneelock, my champ-of-all-champs, will now tussle
And wrestle a beast called the Grizzly-Ghastly
And slap him around! Then he'll slam him down fastly
And pin both his shoulders tight flat to the mat.
Kid Sneelock will love it! I'm sure about that.

And while THAT goes on THERE, look at THIS go on HERE!
Have you heard of my herd of "Through-Horns-Jumping-Deer"...?
Every deer jumps through horns of another pell-mell
While *his* horns are jumped through at the same time as well
By a deer whose horns ALSO are being jumped through
By another who's having HIS horns jumped through, too,
Which I'm *sure* Trainer Sneelock can train them to do.

Then the whole tent will ring with hoorays and wild shouts
When I wheel in my whales and they turn on their spouts!
First my Whale Number One, with an aim that aims true
Spouts a spout that spouts Sneelock to Whale Number Two!
And then Whale Number Two spouts his spout like a gun
And *that* spout spouts old Sneelock right back to Whale One!
And then forwards and backwards on spout after spout
My great Spout-Rider Sneelock gets spouted about
Just as long as the water they're spouting holds out!

Then my Tournament Knights! Noble apes without fears!
Sir Hector! Sir Vector! Sir Bopps! And Sir Beers!
Sir Hawkins! Sir Dawkins! Sir Jawks! And Sir Jeers!
Clatter into the tent, and while everyone cheers
Stage a roust-about-joust with their boxing glove spears!

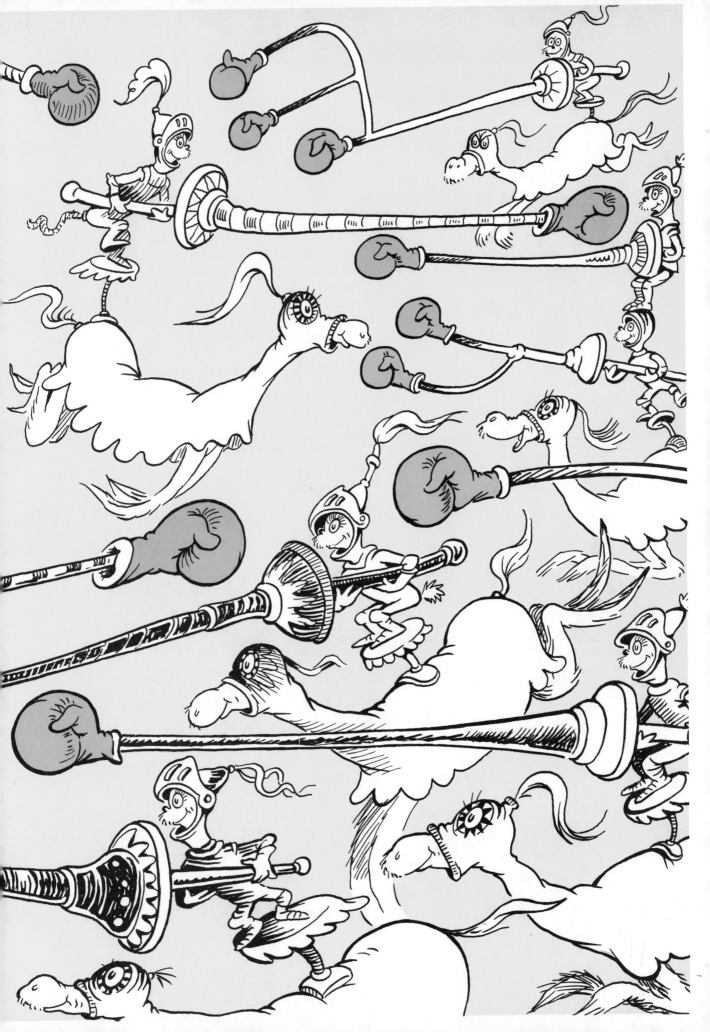

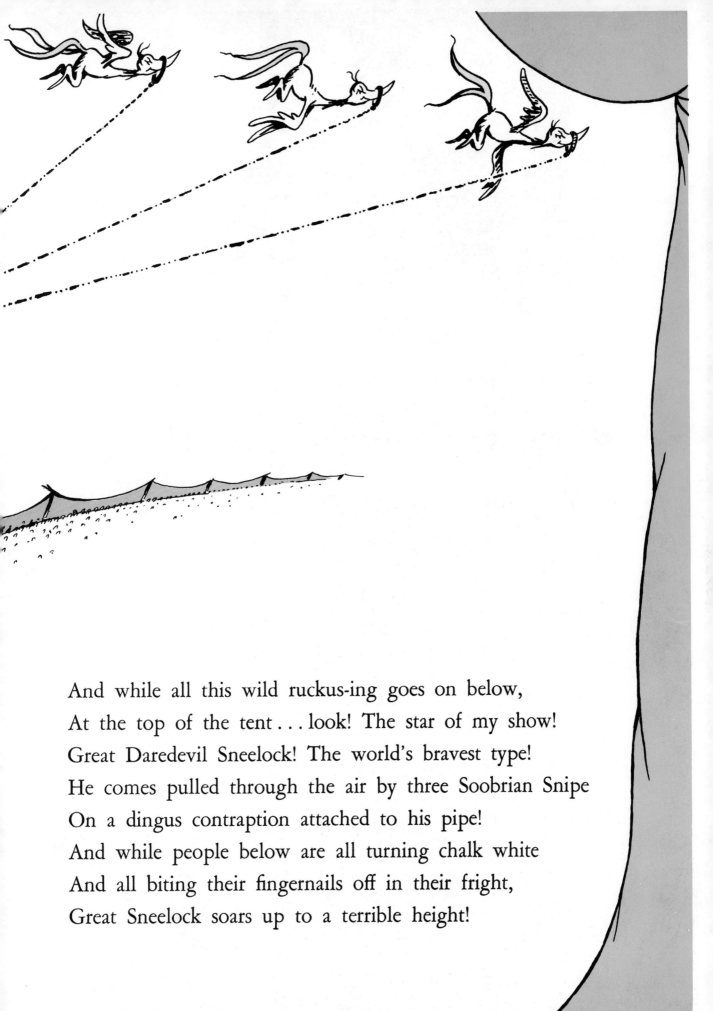

And while all this wild ruckus-ing goes on below,
At the top of the tent . . . look! The star of my show!
Great Daredevil Sneelock! The world's bravest type!
He comes pulled through the air by three Soobrian Snipe
On a dingus contraption attached to his pipe!
And while people below are all turning chalk white
And all biting their fingernails off in their fright,
Great Sneelock soars up to a terrible height!

Then he shakes himself loose!
He starts down in a dive
Such as no man on earth
Could come out of alive!
But he smiles as he falls
And no fear does he feel.
His nerves are like iron,
His muscles like steel.
And he plunges! Down! Down!
With his hair still combed neat
Four thousand, six hundred
And ninety-two feet!

Then he'll land in a fish bowl.
He'll manage just fine.
Don't ask *how* he'll manage.
That's *his* job. Not mine.

Why! He'll be a Hero!
Of *course* he won't mind
When he finds that he has
A big circus behind.

IF I RAN
The ZOO

By Dr. Seuss

RANDOM HOUSE · NEW YORK

For TONI *and*
MICHAEL GORDON TACKABERRY THOMPSON

"It's a pretty good zoo,"
Said young Gerald McGrew,
"And the fellow who runs it
Seems proud of it, too."

"But if *I* ran the zoo,"
Said young Gerald McGrew,
"I'd make a few changes.
That's just what I'd do . . ."

The lions and tigers and that kind of stuff
They have up here now are not *quite* good enough.
You see things like these in just any old zoo.
They're awfully old-fashioned. I want something *new!*

So I'd open each cage. I'd unlock every pen,
Let the animals go, and start over again.
And, somehow or other, I think I could find
Some beasts of a much more un-usual kind.

A *four*-footed lion's not much of a beast.
The one in my zoo will have *ten* feet, at least!
Five legs on the left and five more on the right.
Then people will stare and they'll say, "What a sight!
This Zoo Keeper, New Keeper Gerald's quite keen.
That's the gol-darndest lion I ever have seen!"

My New Zoo, McGrew Zoo, will make people talk.
My New Zoo, McGrew Zoo, will make people gawk
At the strangest odd creatures that ever did walk.
I'll get, for my zoo, a new sort-of-a-hen
Who roosts in another hen's topknot, and *then*
Another one roosts in the topknot of his,
And another in *his,* and another in HIS,
And so forth and upward and onward, gee whizz!

But that's just a start. I'll do better than *that*.
They'll see me next day, in my zoo-keeper's hat,
Coming into my zoo with an Elephant-Cat!

They'll be so surprised they'll all swallow their gum.
They'll ask, when they see my strange animals come,
"Where *do* you suppose he gets things like that from?
His animals all have such very odd faces.
I'll bet he must hunt them in rather odd places!"

And that's what I'll do,
Said young Gerald McGrew.
If you want to catch beasts you don't see every day,
You have to go places quite out-of-the-way.
You have to go places no others can get to.
You have to get cold and you have to get wet, too.
Up past the North Pole, where the frozen winds squeal,
I'll go and I'll hunt in my Skeegle-mobile
And bring back a family of *What-do-you-know!*
And that's how my New Zoo, McGrew Zoo, will grow.

I'll hunt in the mountains of Zomba-ma-Tant
With helpers who all wear their eyes at a slant,
And capture a fine fluffy bird called the Bustard
Who only eats custard with sauce made of mustard.
And, also, a very fine beast called the Flustard
Who only eats mustard with sauce made of custard.

I'll catch 'em in caves and I'll catch 'em in brooks,
I'll catch 'em in crannies, I'll catch 'em in nooks
That you don't read about in geography books.

I'll catch 'em in countries that no one can spell
Like the country of Motta-fa-Potta-fa-Pell.
In a country like that, if a hunter is clever,
He'll hunt up some beasts that you never saw ever!

I'll load up five boats with a family of Joats
Whose feet are like cows', but wear squirrel-skin coats
And sit down like dogs, but have voices like goats —
Excepting they can't sing the very high notes.

And then I'll go down to the Wilds of Nantucket
And capture a family of Lunks in a bucket.
Then people will say, "Now I like that boy heaps.
His New Zoo, McGrew Zoo, is growing by leaps.
He captures them wild and he captures them meek,
He captures them slim and he captures them sleek.
What *do* you suppose he will capture next week?"

I'll capture one tiny. I'll capture one cute.
I'll capture a deer that no hunter would shoot.
A deer that's so nice he could sleep in your bed
If it weren't for those horns that he has on his head.

And speaking of horns that are just a bit queer,
I'll bring back a very odd family of deer:
A father, a mother, two sisters, a brother
Whose horns are connected, from one to the other,
Whose horns are so mixed they can't tell them apart,
Can't tell where they end and can't tell where they start!
Each deer's mighty puzzled. He's never yet found
If *his* horns are *hers,* or the other way 'round.

I'll capture them fat and I'll capture them scrawny.
I'll capture a scraggle-foot Mulligatawny,
A high-stepping animal fast as the wind
From the blistering sands of the Desert of Zind.
This beast is the beast that the brave chieftains ride
When they want to go fast to find some place to hide.
A Mulligatawny is fine for my zoo
And so is a chieftain. I'll bring one back, too.

In the Far Western part
Of south-east North Dakota
Lives a very fine animal
Called the Iota.
But I'll capture one
Who is even much finer
In the north-eastern west part
Of South Carolina.

When people see *him,* they will say, "Now, by thunder!
This New Zoo, McGrew Zoo, is really a wonder!"

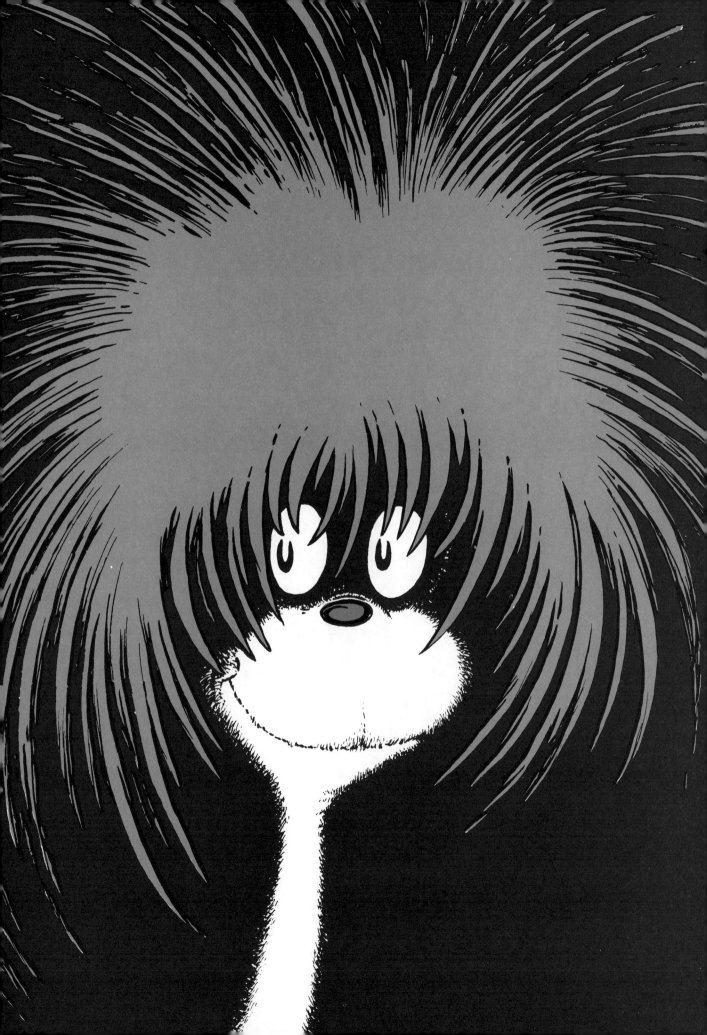

Most beasts are quite friendly, but still, in some lands
Some beasts are too dangerous to catch with bare hands.
For those that are ugly and vicious and mean
I'll build a Bad-Animal-Catching-Machine.
It's rather expensive to build such a kit,
But with it a hunter can never get bit.

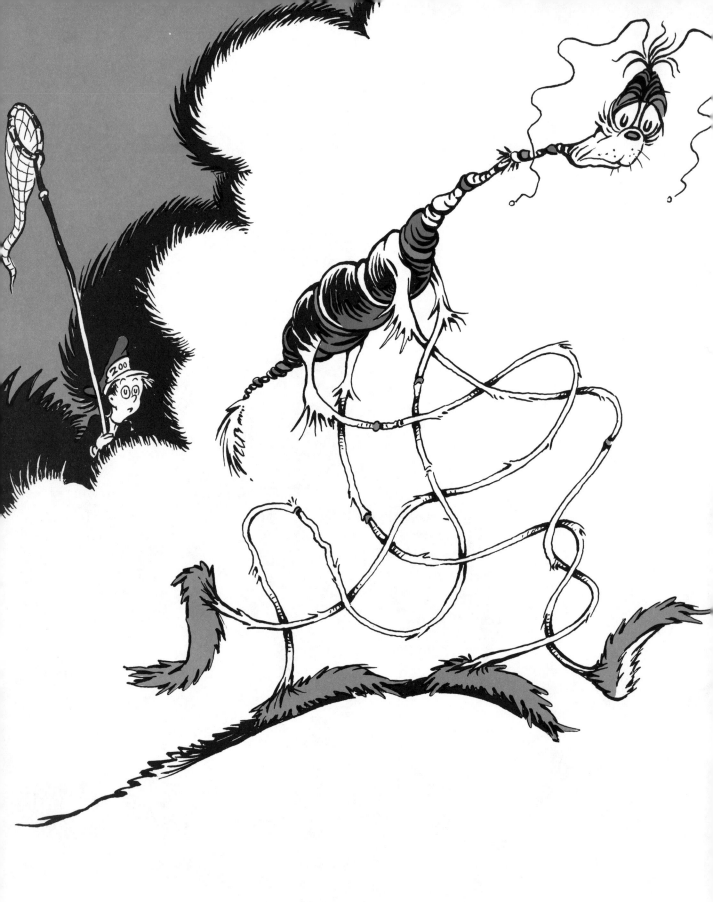

A zoo should have bugs, so I'll capture a Thwerll
Whose legs are snarled up in a terrible snerl.

And then I'll go out and I'll capture some Chuggs,
Some keen-shooter, mean-shooter, bean-shooter bugs.

I'll go to the African island of Yerka
And bring back a tizzle-topped Tufted Mazurka,
A kind of canary with quite a tall throat.
His neck is so long, if he swallows an oat
For breakfast the first day of April, they say
It has to go down such a very long way
That it gets to his stomach the fifteenth of May.

I'll bag a big bug
Who is very surprising,
A feller who has
A propeller for rising
And zooming around
Making cross-country hops,
From Texas to Boston
With only two stops.
Now *that* sort of thing
For a bug is just tops!

And when I've caught *him,*
Then the next thing you know
I'll go and I'll capture
A wild Tick-Tack-Toe,
With X's that win
And with Zeros that lose.
He'll look mighty good
In this Zoo of McGrew's.

I'll bring back a Gusset, a Gherkin, a Gasket
And also a Gootch from the wilds of Nantasket.

And eight Persian Princes will carry the basket,
But what *their* names are, I don't know. So don't ask it.

In a cave in Kartoom lives a beast called the Natch
That no other hunter's been able to catch.
He's hidden for years in his cave with a pout
And no one's been able to make him come out.
But *I'll* coax him out with a wonderful meal
That's cooked by my cooks in my Cooker-mobile.

They'll fix up a dish that is just to his taste;
Three chicken croquettes made of library paste,
Then sprinkled with peanut shucks, pickled and spiced,
Then baked at 600 degrees and then iced.
It's mighty hard cooking to cook up such feasts
But that's how the New Zoo, McGrew Zoo, gets beasts.

I'll go to the far-away Mountains of Tobsk
Near the River of Nobsk, and I'll bring back an Obsk,
A sort of a kind of a Thing-a-ma-Bobsk
Who only eats rhubarb and corn-on-the-cobsk.
Then people will flock to my zoo in a mobsk.
"McGrew," they will say, "does a wonderful jobsk!
He hunts with such vim and he hunts with such vigor,
His New Zoo, McGrew Zoo, gets bigger and bigger!"

And, speaking of birds, there's the Russian Palooski,
Whose headski is redski and belly is blueski.
I'll get one of *them* for my Zooski McGrewski.

Then the whole town will gasp, "Why, this boy never sleeps!
No keeper before ever kept what *he* keeps!
There's no telling WHAT that young fellow will do!"
And then, just to show them, I'll sail to Ka-Troo
          And

                    Bring

                    Back

an IT-KUTCH

a PREEP

and a PROO

a NERKLE

a NERD

and a SEERSUCKER, too!

I'll hunt in the Jungles of Hippo-no-Hungus
And bring back a flock of wild Bippo-no-Bungus!
The Bippo-no-Bungus from Hippo-no-Hungus
Are better than those down in Dippo-no-Dungus
And smarter than those out in Nippo-no-Nungus.
And that's why I'll catch 'em in Hippo-no-Hungus
Instead of those others in Nungus and Dungus.
And people will say when they see these Bips bounding,
"This Zoo Keeper, New Keeper's simply astounding!
He travels so far that you'd think he would drop!
When *do* you suppose this young fellow will stop?"

Stop . . . ?
Well, I should.
But I won't stop until
I've captured the Fizza-ma-Wizza-ma-Dill,
The world's biggest bird from the Island of Gwark
Who only eats pine trees and spits out the bark.
And boy! When I get *him* back home to my park,
The whole *world* will say, "Young McGrew's made his mark.
He's built a zoo better than Noah's whole Ark!
These wonderful, marvelous beasts that he chooses
Have made him the greatest of all the McGrewses!"

"WOW!" They'll all cheer,
"What this zoo must be worth!
It's the gol-darndest zoo
On the face of the earth!"

"Yes . . .
That's what I'd do,"
Said young Gerald McGrew.
"I'd make a few changes
If *I* ran the zoo."

THEODOR SEUSS GEISEL, known to his millions of fans as Dr. Seuss, wrote and illustrated forty-three books. He forever changed the face of children's literature in 1937 with his first book, *And to Think That I Saw It on Mulberry Street*. His last, *Oh, the Places You'll Go!*, was on the *New York Times* bestseller list without interruption for over two years. He was credited with bringing fun into the process of learning to read after he launched Beginner Books with *The Cat in the Hat* in 1957.

Long considered a national treasure, Dr. Seuss was awarded a Pulitzer Prize Special Citation in 1984. He received virtually every children's book award, including the Laura Ingalls Wilder Award and three Caldecott Honors for *McElligot's Pool, Bartholomew and the Oobleck*, and *If I Ran the Zoo*. In addition, he earned two Emmys and a Peabody Award for his animated television specials.

Dr. Seuss was born in Springfield, Massachusetts, on March 2, 1904, and died at his home in La Jolla, California, on September 24, 1991.

Books written and illustrated by Dr. Seuss:

AND TO THINK THAT I SAW IT ON MULBERRY STREET
THE 500 HATS OF BARTHOLOMEW CUBBINS
THE KING'S STILTS
HORTON HATCHES THE EGG
McELLIGOT'S POOL
THIDWICK THE BIG-HEARTED MOOSE
BARTHOLOMEW AND THE OOBLECK
IF I RAN THE ZOO
SCRAMBLED EGGS SUPER!
HORTON HEARS A WHO!
ON BEYOND ZEBRA
IF I RAN THE CIRCUS
HOW THE GRINCH STOLE CHRISTMAS!
YERTLE THE TURTLE AND OTHER STORIES
HAPPY BIRTHDAY TO YOU!
THE SNEETCHES AND OTHER STORIES
DR. SEUSS'S SLEEP BOOK
I HAD TROUBLE IN GETTING TO SOLLA SOLLEW
THE CAT IN THE HAT SONGBOOK
I CAN LICK 30 TIGERS TODAY! AND OTHER STORIES
I CAN DRAW IT MYSELF
THE LORAX
DID I EVER TELL YOU HOW LUCKY YOU ARE?
HUNCHES IN BUNCHES
THE BUTTER BATTLE BOOK
YOU'RE ONLY OLD ONCE!
OH, THE PLACES YOU'LL GO!

Beginner Books
THE CAT IN THE HAT
THE CAT IN THE HAT COMES BACK
ONE FISH TWO FISH RED FISH BLUE FISH
GREEN EGGS AND HAM
HOP ON POP
DR. SEUSS'S ABC
FOX IN SOCKS
THE FOOT BOOK
MR. BROWN CAN MOO! CAN YOU?
MARVIN K. MOONEY WILL YOU PLEASE GO NOW!
THE SHAPE OF ME AND OTHER STUFF
THERE'S A WOCKET IN MY POCKET!
OH, THE THINKS YOU CAN THINK!
THE CAT'S QUIZZER
I CAN READ WITH MY EYES SHUT!
OH SAY CAN YOU SAY?